RAPUNZEL

WHEN SHE WAS TWELVE YEARS OLD THE WITCH TOOK HER DEEP INTO THE FOREST

RAPUNZEL

From The Brothers Grimm
retold by
Barbara Rogasky
with illustrations by
Trina Schart Hyman

Holiday House
New York

for Karleen
T.S.H.

for
Dorothy Ludwig
B.R.

Library of Congress Cataloging in Publication Data

Rogasky, Barbara.
    Rapunzel.

    Summary: Retells the tale of the beautiful girl
imprisoned in a lonely tower by a witch.
    [1. Fairy tales.   2. Folklore—Germany]
I. Hyman, Trina Schart, ill.   II. Grimm, Jakob,
1785–1863. Rapunzel.   III. Title.
PZ8.R618Rap   398.2′1′0943 [E]   81–6419
ISBN 0–8234–0454–4   AACR2

Once upon a time, long ago, a husband and wife lived together in a cottage in the woods. Their life was poor but happy, and for many years they yearned for a child of their own. At long last, the wife learned she was going to have a baby, and she and her husband were filled with great joy.

Now, at the back of their house was a small window that looked out over a magical and wonderful garden. Every day the woman would stand on a stool and peer out at the delicious-looking vegetables and beautiful flowers. But she could never do anything except look, because the garden was surrounded by a high stone wall. Besides, the garden was owned by a witch who was very old and very powerful. Her name was Mother Gothel, and she was so feared that even people who had never seen her had nightmares about her.

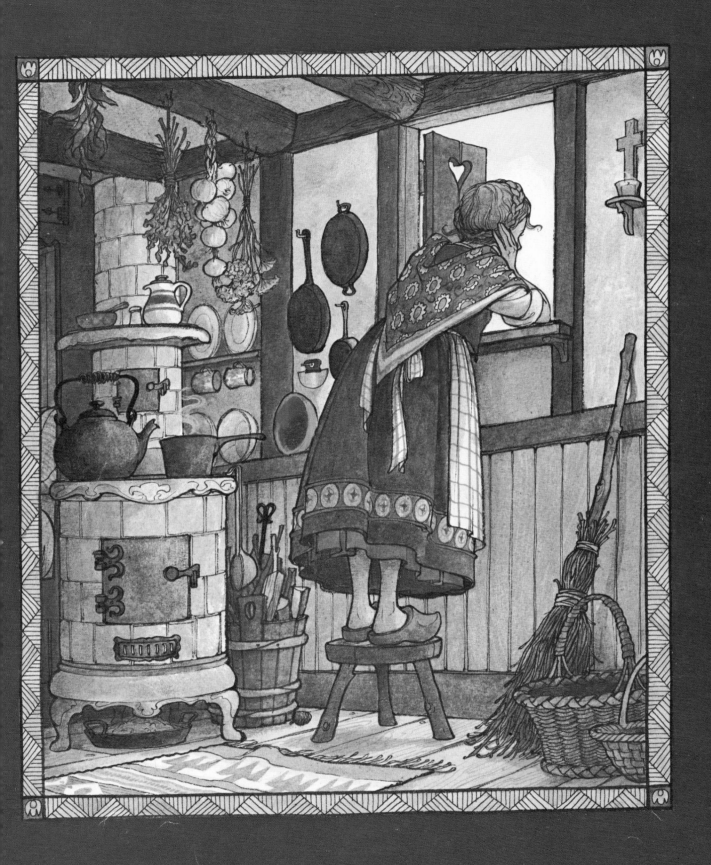

Day after day, the woman would climb on the stool and look out the window at the garden. She noticed that in the very center there was a patch of rampion, which some people used in salads. After that, no matter where she looked, her eyes came back to the rampion. She desperately wanted to taste it for herself.

The yearning grew, and before long all she could think about was the wonderful salad that the rampion would make. She spent more and more of her time staring out of the tiny window. She stopped eating, because nothing could taste as good to her as a salad made from the rampion in the witch's garden. Soon she grew thin and weak, and she could barely climb onto the stool to look out of the window.

"I know it," she said, her voice getting weaker and weaker. "But I think I shall die unless I can have some of that rampion."

The man loved his wife very much. He patted her hand. "Don't worry," he said. "I'll find a way."

Her husband had noticed all of this, and he was half mad with worry.

"My wife," he said to her, "what is the matter with you? Our baby will be here soon, and you are too thin and frail to give it birth. What is wrong?"

"Ah, husband," she sighed, "I want what I cannot have."

"What is that?" he asked. He had to lean forward to hear her, so weak had her voice become.

"The rampion," she replied.

"Is that all?" He leaped up, ready to get her some.

She shook her head. "The rampion from the witch's garden."

Her husband sat back down. "But no one can get into that garden!"

He thought and he thought, and he finally said to himself, "What else can I do? I cannot let her die. No matter how dangerous it is, I'll have to get her some of the rampion."

So that night, gathering his courage about him, he climbed over the wall, quickly pulled up some of the plants, and quietly climbed back home again.

His wife was so overjoyed, she hardly stopped to thank him. She made an enormous salad with the rampion, and ate every bite.

That finished the rampion. There was not a single piece left. The very next day, she began to yearn for more. Once again, she stopped eating and kept staring out of the window at the witch's rampion. Once more she grew thin and weak, barely able to climb onto the stool.

Her husband did not wait long this time. He had succeeded once, and he would do it a second time. He resolved to get her what she craved. After dark, he climbed over the high wall and went straight to the patch of rampion.

But now the witch stood there, waiting for him. Hate gleamed from her eyes. "Thief! Foul thief! How dare you sneak into my garden and steal my rampion! Now I will have to punish you!"

The husband shook so much from fright that he almost could not speak. "Oh, Mother Gothel, please!" he begged. "Don't hurt me! It wasn't my fault. I did it for my wife. She saw your beautiful rampion from our window, and now it's all she can think of. She won't eat anything else. I'm afraid she'll die and take our unborn child with her. I would never have done it otherwise. Please don't hurt me!"

When the witch heard of an unborn child, the evil fell away from her face. "I won't harm you," she said to the husband. "You can take as much of the rampion as you need to keep your wife well. But you have to promise me one thing."

"Anything, anything!" the husband cried.

"Swear that when your child is born, if it is a daughter, you will give her to me," the witch said.

Like a rabbit frozen with fear, the husband agreed, and the witch sent him home with an armful of rampion.

When Rapunzel was twelve years old, the witch took her deep into the forest to a place where a tall tower stood, surrounded by thorns. High at the very top was a small room with just one window. The witch shut Rapunzel inside, and then sealed up the door and took down the stairs.

On the very day the woman gave birth to a girl child, the witch appeared. She took the baby from her cradle and said, "I will name you Rapunzel," which meant rampion in their country. Then, paying no attention to the tears and cries of the baby's father and mother, she left the cottage with the infant girl in her arms.

The witch was never unkind to Rapunzel. Indeed, she gave her almost everything the child could have wished for. And Rapunzel grew to be the most beautiful child in the world. She had long blonde hair, as thick and glowing as sunlight or beaten gold.

In the room Rapunzel stayed, locked away from the world. She saw no one but her witch-mother, and nothing of the outside except the view from her window.

The witch came to see her once or twice a week. She would stand outside the tower and call:

"Rapunzel, Rapunzel,
Let down your hair."

And Rapunzel would loosen the thick braids from her head, wind them around the window latch, and drop them down the long distance to the witch standing below. Mother Gothel would climb up the braids to the window, using Rapunzel's hair as a ladder.

Several years passed this way, with Rapunzel locked in the tower and the witch using her braids to climb into the room.

One afternoon, when the prince stood listening, Mother Gothel came. He quickly hid behind some trees where she could not see him. He heard her call out:

"Rapunzel, Rapunzel,
Let down your hair."

He watched, amazed, as Rapunzel let down her hair and the witch climbed up to the top of the tower.

"So that's how it's done," he said. "Tomorrow, I shall do the same thing."

One day, the king's son was riding through the forest. He heard Rapunzel's sweet, lonely voice singing a song that pierced his heart. He rode hither and yon until he found the tower, but try as he might he could find no way to get inside. When night fell, he left the forest and rode home, but he could not forget the beauty of Rapunzel's voice. The next day, he returned to the tower to hear it once more. The song was as lovely as he remembered, and so he came back every day to hear Rapunzel's voice again and again.

The next day at sundown, he stood at the foot of the tower and called out:

"Rapunzel, Rapunzel,
Let down your hair."

And down tumbled the thick golden hair. He climbed up swiftly and entered the room through the small window.

Rapunzel was terribly frightened when she saw him. She had been expecting Mother Gothel. Besides, she had never in her life seen a man before. But the prince calmed her by speaking gently and kindly to her. He told her he had heard her lovely song, and that it had touched him so deeply he could not rest until he had seen her. At that Rapunzel smiled, and her fear of him disappeared.

The smile made Rapunzel even more beautiful. The prince fell in love with her then and there and embraced her tenderly. He pleaded with her to be his wife and to come away with him to his father's kingdom.

Rapunzel thought carefully before she answered. "He is certainly better looking than Mother Gothel," she said to herself, "and he's nicer too. Mother Gothel never says such sweet things to me!"

To the king's son she said, "Prince, I would gladly be your wife and come away with you. But as you see, I am locked up in this room. You can help me. Each time you come, bring a skein of silk with you. I'll weave a strong ladder out of it, and climb down on that. Then we can go together to your kingdom. But you must promise me," she warned him, "to come only in the evenings. Mother Gothel visits during the day."

The prince agreed. Thereafter, every time he came to see Rapunzel, he called out:

"Rapunzel, Rapunzel,
Let down your hair."

And he climbed up her braids, each time carrying a skein of silk.

Slowly and secretly, Rapunzel wove the silk into a ladder strong enough to hold her own weight.

After some time, the ladder was almost finished, and Mother Gothel still knew nothing. But one day, when Rapunzel had watched the witch make her clumsy climb to the tower room, the girl forgot her secret.

"Mother Gothel," she said, "how is it that it takes you so long to climb up here when the king's son does it so fast?"

"Oh, wretched girl!" The witch flew into a rage. "Wicked, ungrateful child! I thought I had hidden you from all the world. I thought I had given you all your heart could desire. And now you have betrayed me!"

In her great fury she snatched a pair of scissors and cut Rapunzel's braids from her head. Then, using the secret silken ladder to descend from the tower, she took Rapunzel deeper still into the woods to a cold and desolate place and left her there, to live or die in loneliness and misery.

The witch returned to the tower immediately, pulling the ladder up behind her. At dusk, she heard the prince call:

"Rapunzel, Rapunzel,
Let down your hair."

The witch wrapped Rapunzel's hair on the window latch and dropped the braids down to the prince. As usual, thinking nothing amiss, he climbed up to the tower room.

But instead of his beautiful wife—for by that time, they had married—he saw a hideous witch, evil shooting from her eyes like flames.

"Thief!" she hissed. "Foul thief! You have come to see your darling, your beautiful songbird, have you? The cat got her—yes, the cat got her, and she will never sing again. And, my handsome, sneaking lad, that same cat will get your eyes. I swear you will never see Rapunzel again. Never!"

The prince was frozen with fear and mad with grief. He backed away from Mother Gothel's awful rage without thinking, and fell out of the window.

He did not die, however. The thorn bushes at the bottom of the tower acted like a cushion and saved his life. But the thorns put out his eyes and blinded him. He could see no more.

For a year he wandered like a homeless beggar in the forest, lamenting the loss of his love Rapunzel. The tears from his sightless eyes gave salt to the roots and berries he ate to stay alive.

Because he could not see, the prince never knew where he was or whether it was day or night. One day, at sundown, he happened to pass the barren place where Rapunzel lived now with the twins she had borne. She was singing, as she often did, to ease her loneliness and to soothe the babies.

The prince heard her voice and knew it was Rapunzel. With the faltering steps of a blind man, he sought out the place where Rapunzel sang and fell on his knees before her. Despite his changed appearance, Rapunzel knew him instantly. Her happiness was so great at the sight of him, she could not speak. She threw her arms around his neck and wept for joy.

Her tears flowed into the prince's eyes, and they cleared. He saw light, and then his beloved Rapunzel. He could see again, as well as he ever had before.

Carrying the twins, they left the bare and desolate place in the forest forever.

They returned to the prince's kingdom, and there they lived happily together for many long and loving years.